EASTER EGG HUNT

Easter is here, and the egg hunt has started!
Read closely, as this will be a very special event.

Egg hunt? I need to get my **bricks** together on the next comic page and start searching!

Let's hop from one **activity** to another in pursuit of the egg!

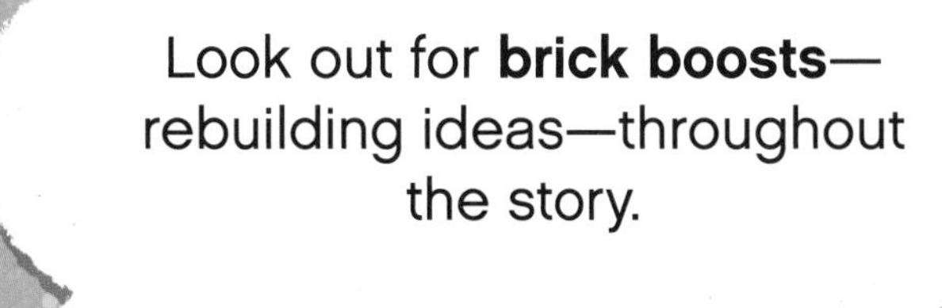

Let the race begin!

STARRING:

EGGWARD

The elusive egg!

Hopper

The brisk bunny!

Baasil

The leisurely lamb!

BUILD ME!

EGGWARD

One spring morning, Eggward was getting ready to go out. He checked his neatly painted stripes and stepped outside.

What a lovely day!
Perfect for a walk to the egg-gathering spot.

Egg hunt is ON!
Bunny going into action!

That bunny is following me again. This happens every year!
Time for the escape plan.

Where is he?
He was right here!

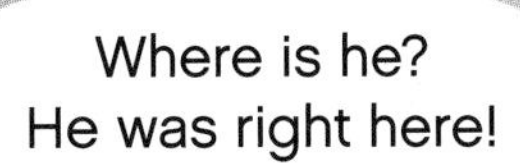

Too many stripes!
Too many stripes!
I'm getting dizzy . . .

Works every time!

Hopper is not giving up! Untangle the lines to help Eggward find a path to the pond.

Answer on page 47.

Eggward needs to hide, so he builds a snorkel and jumps into the pond. Can you find the yellow fish who will help him get to the other side?

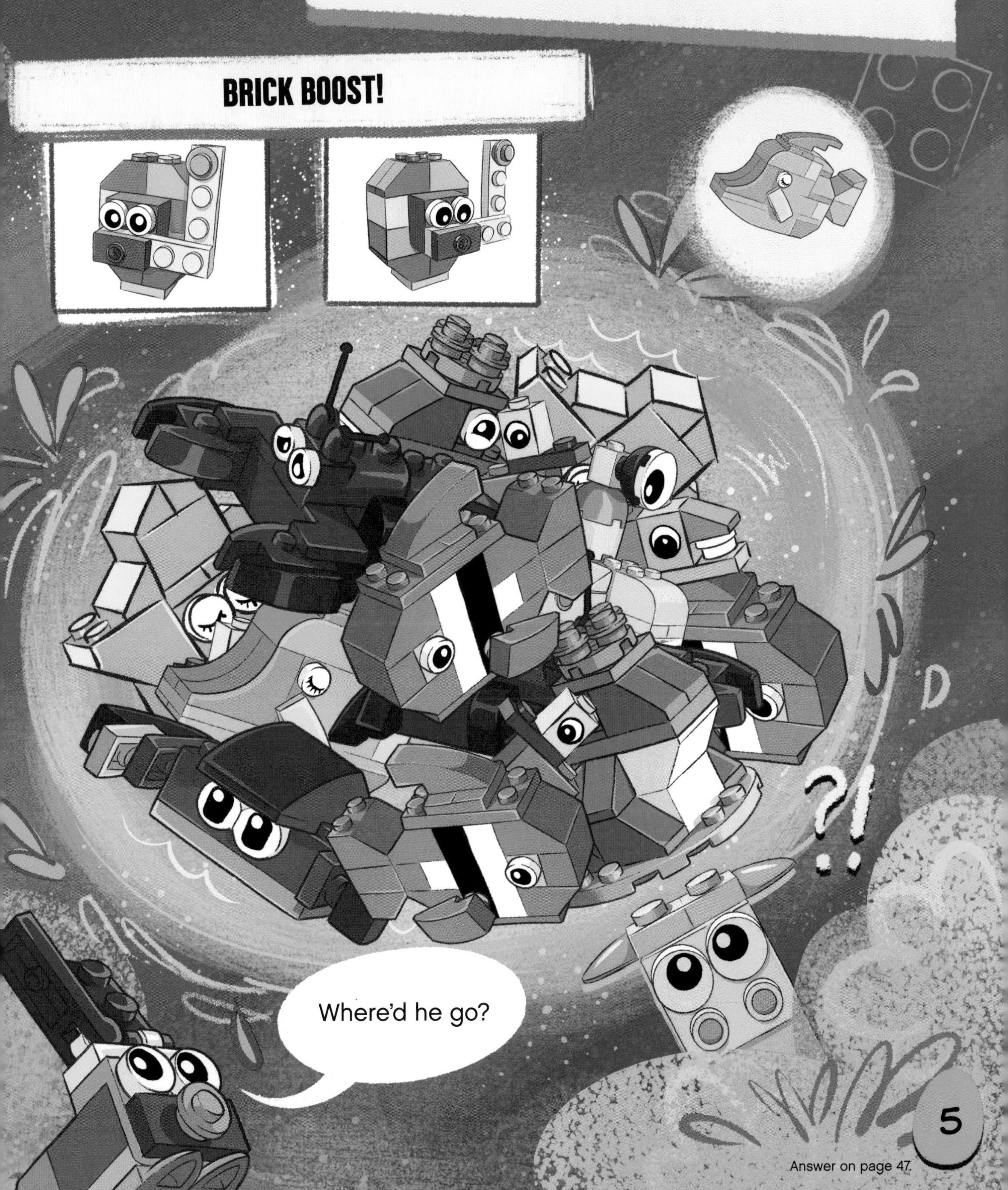

Answer on page 47.

After the dive, Eggward takes off his mask and finds his colors were washed off! Draw some new disguises for him to try.

Quick! There's a hedge Eggward can hide behind. Mark the hole he can pass through!

Answer on page 47.

Now Eggward needs to reach that house. Help him cross the muddy garden by stepping only on egg-shaped rocks.

Answer on page 47.

Look at the Easter feast and circle the things that don't belong. Then, draw Eggward running on the table!

Answers on page 47.

Hopper is close, and Eggward needs to take cover! Connect the dots to see where Eggward is hiding.

Time for a sweet break! Draw the treats in the empty spaces so that there is only one of each treat in every row and column.

Answers on page 47.

Where's that clever egg now? Find him, then look at the smaller pieces and put a check mark by the one that doesn't match the big picture.

Answers on page 47.

Eggward jumps under the table and finds lots of bunnies! He's a quick thinker, so he puts on bunny ears. Can you spot him now?

BRICK BOOST!

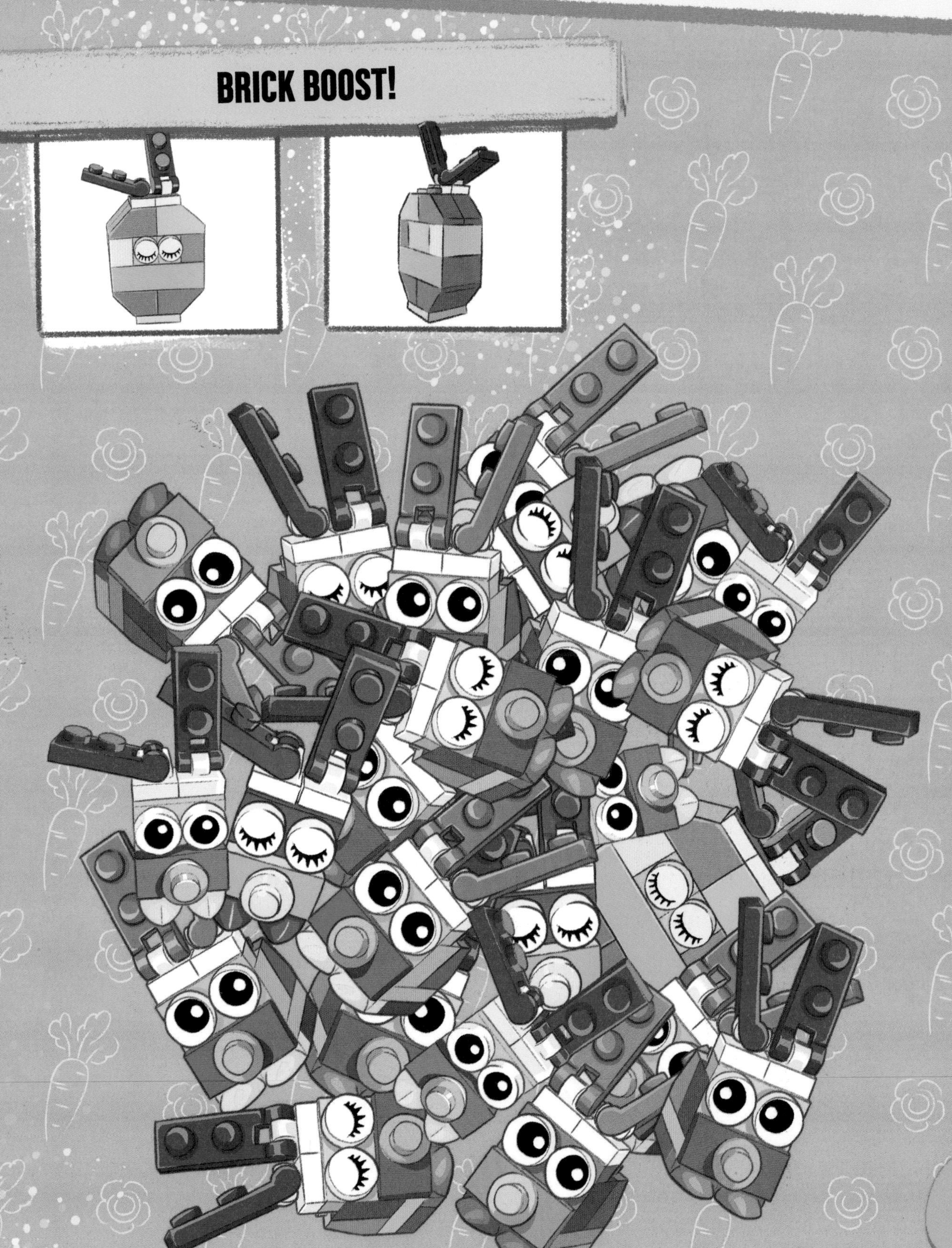

Answer on page 47.

Eggward escapes outside, straight into the garden next door. Help him find his way out while collecting all the flowers on the way.

Answer on page 47.

Beyond the garden, Eggward finds a river. The egg takes off the bunny ears and builds a canoe. Which of his reflections in the water is the right one?

Answer on page 47.

Chocolate factory ahead! Eggward jumps out of the canoe and runs inside the building, straight into a stream of chocolate! Find chocolate-covered Eggward among the other treats.

Answer on page 47.

Eggward's chocolate coating starts to fall off. Match the pieces with the right places.

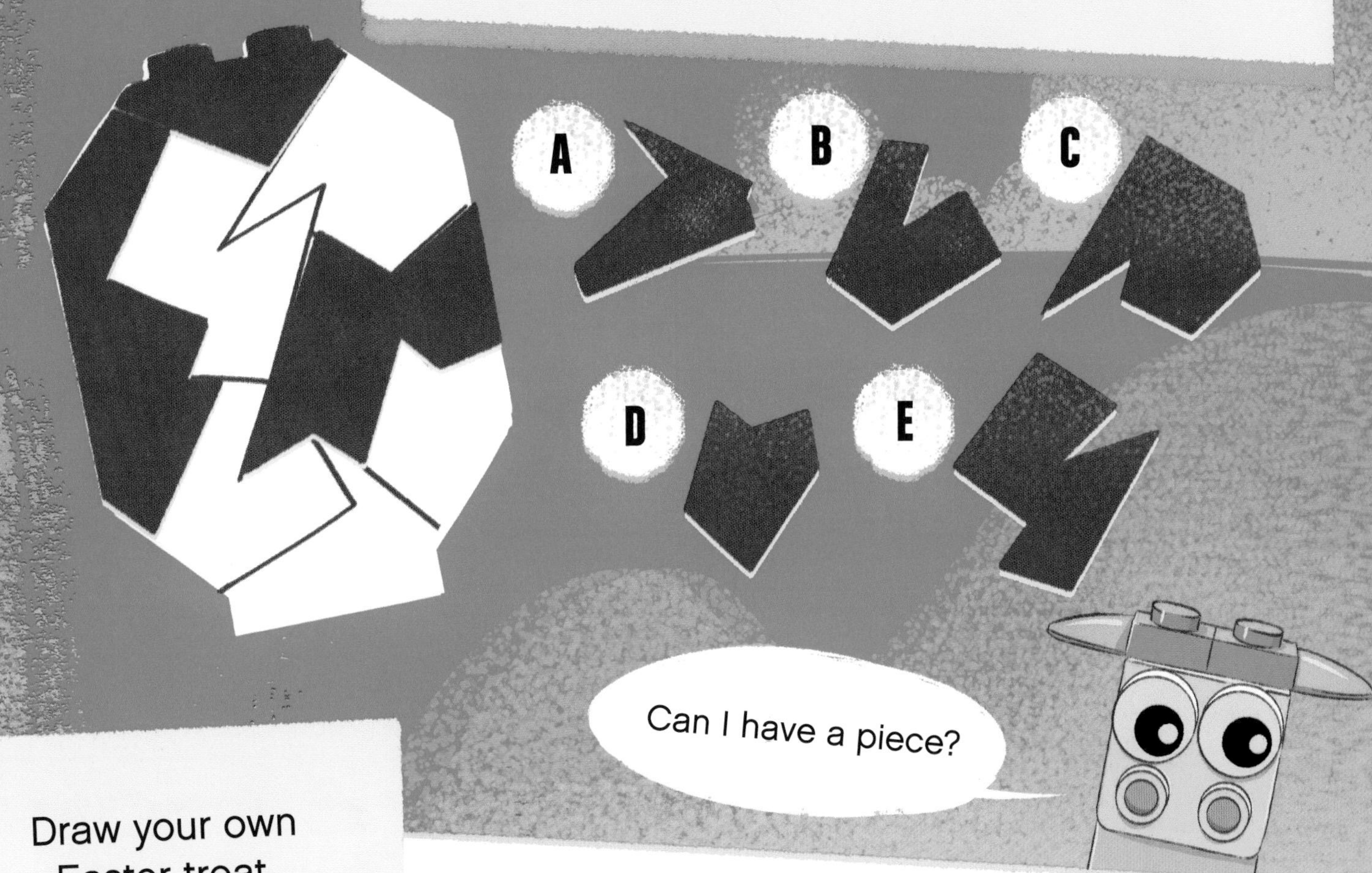

Draw your own Easter treat.

Answers on page 47.

Time to fly! Eggward builds a turbo jetpack.
Untangle the flight paths to help Eggward reach the basket.

Answer on page 47.

The egg has landed! But Baasil and Hopper are in the basket too. Write their coordinates in the boxes below.

Answers on page 47.

BUILD ME!
HOPPER
After getting out of the basket, Hopper lost sight of Eggward. She decided to ask around about him.
Have you seen an egg? Stripes, colorful, big eyes.
Woof! Sorry!
I'm looking for a painted Easter egg.
Whooo, there are lots there.
How can I explain what egg I am looking for if there are so many?
Baaad luck! Maybe draw a picture?
Has anyone seen this egg?
That's an egg? I thought it was a potato.

Hopper announces a wanted poster contest! Find the poster that shows Eggward correctly and color it in.

Answer on page 47.

Hopper builds herself a hoverboard to continue the chase. Which shadow belongs to the boarding bunny?

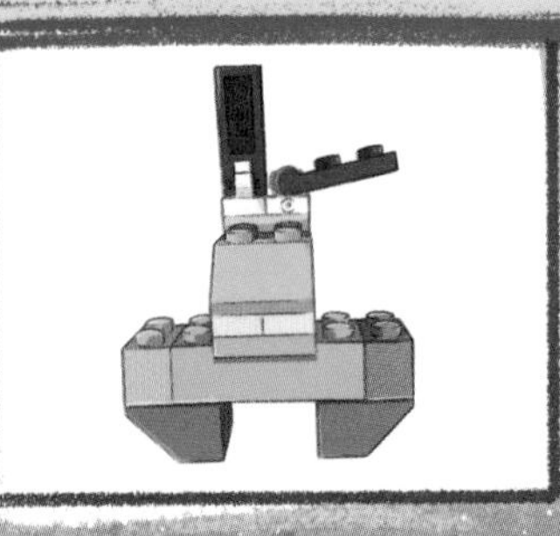

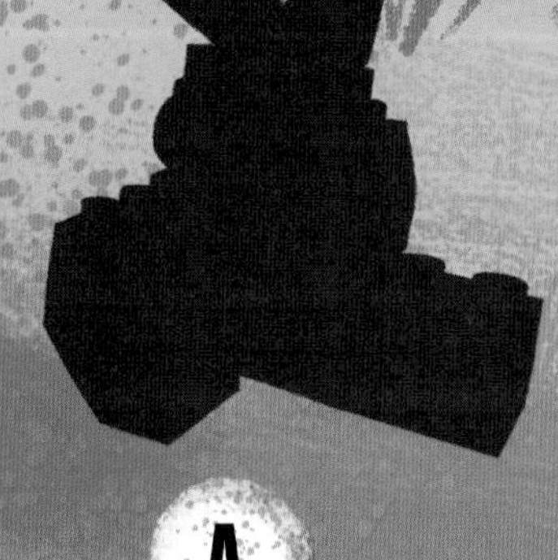

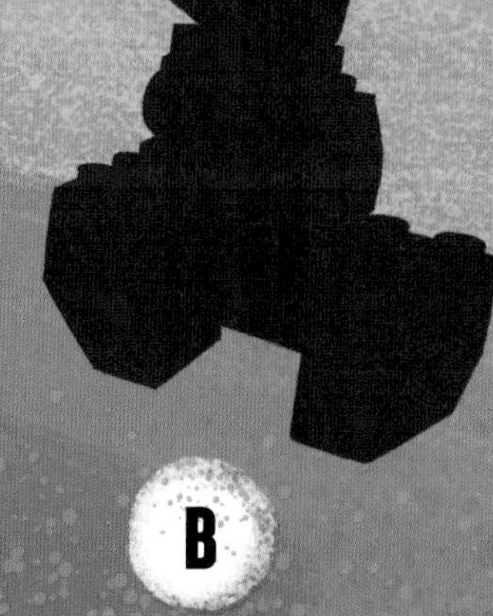

Answer on page 47.

Quick! Help the impatient bunny find a way out of the maze by only following the Easter objects across and down.

Hey, wait up!

Answer on page 47.

From her hoverboard, Hopper can see a few Easter baskets.
Count them and write the number in the box below.
Can you spot Eggward too?

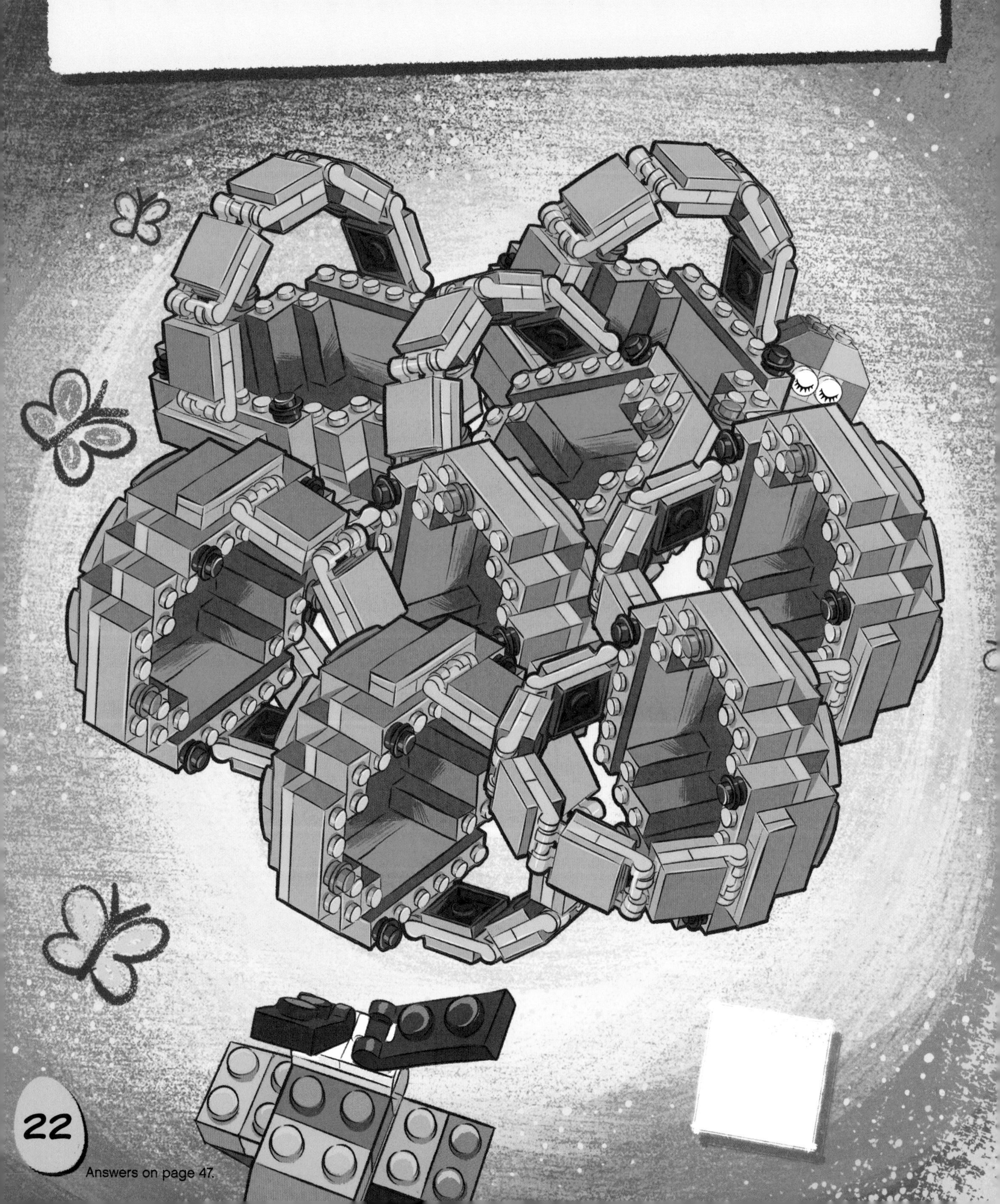

Answers on page 47.

Hopper ditches the hoverboard and builds wings to follow Eggward. But the bunny starts flying upside down! Color the image of Hopper flying right-side up.

BRICK BOOST!

Where did the basket with Eggward go? Hopper isn't sure.
Untangle the ribbons to help her figure it out.
Mark the right answer in the boxes below.

Answer on page 48.

Hopper senses the egg is near and builds herself some binoculars. Look at the close-ups below and mark the ones you can find in the big picture.

BRICK BOOST!

Answers on page 48.

Continuing the chase, the bunny flies into a room full of toys! Circle the odd one out on each shelf.

Answers on page 48.

Hopper almost catches up with Eggward, so she drops the wings and binoculars. But the situation changes quickly. Circle ten differences between the pictures below.

Answers on page 48.

Dinner time! Hopper builds a carrot picker. Without lifting your pencil, draw a line connecting all the carrots so that Hopper can pick them and share a meal with friends.

Answer on page 48.

Hopper drops the carrot picker for a picture with her bunny friends. Match the pieces below to the picture and write down their coordinates in the boxes.

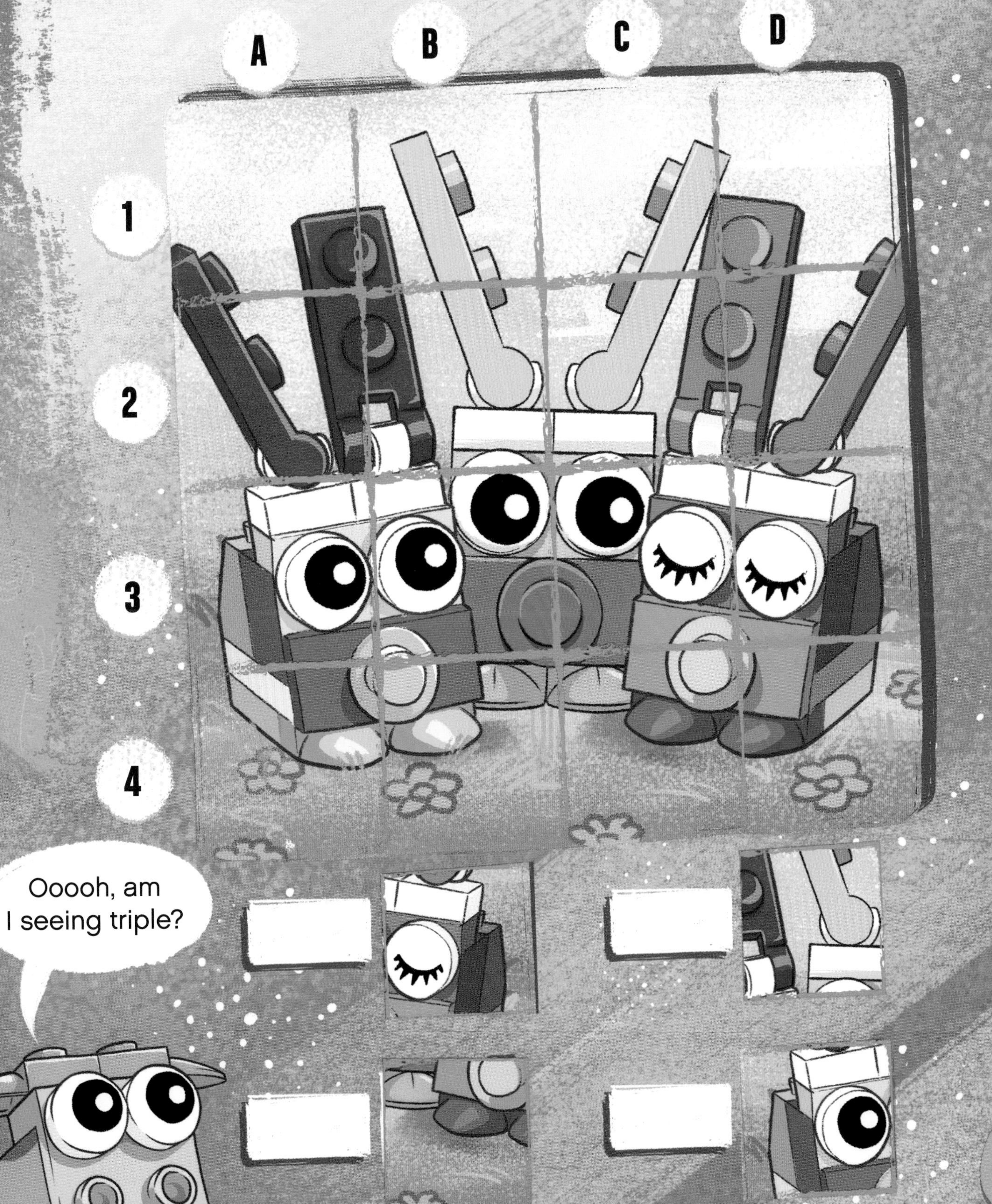

Answers on page 48.

Help Hopper catch up to Eggward. Find each of the three-tile sequences containing Eggward in the grid and draw over them. The remaining squares will create the path Hopper needs to take.

Answer on page 48.

Hopper wants to get back to tracking Eggward. But the bunny is fading after all this hopping around. Help her regain strength by finishing her portrait.

Answer on page 48.

BUILD ME!
BAASIL
After a short break, Hopper is back on Eggward's trail, and Baasil wants to join the fun too!
Hopper! Hopper! Can I play too?
Look at me! Bunny hop!
Oops . . .
Oh no, not again!
Look at me! Bunny bounce!
Whoopsie!
There's only one thing I can do in this difficult situation . . .
. . . hit the hay!

Baasil has woken up! Help the lamb through the haystack by avoiding all the hungry hay bugs.

FINISH

START

Answer on page 48.

Baasil builds enormous ears to listen for Hopper and Eggward. Find out which way to go by circling the melody that has Eggward's favorite note repeated three times.

Answer on page 48.

Answers on page 48.

Baasil sees Hopper and Eggward in the distance. He drops his extra ears and runs! Help Baasil catch up by drawing the lamb's legs in the right positions.

Answers on page 48.

Eggward and Hopper jump over a wall. Baasil wants to follow, so he builds himself longer legs and platform shoes, but—whoops!—he makes a hole in the wall. Which hole was made by the lamb?

Answer on page 48.

There is a beautiful meadow behind the wall. Using the colors of the flowers below, color in the squares to see what picture appears in the meadow.

+	+	+	+	+	+	+	+	+	+	+	+	+
+	+	+	+	+	Δ	Δ	Δ	+	+	+	+	+
+	+	+	+	−	−	−	−	−	+	+	+	+
+	+	+	●	●	●	●	●	●	●	+	+	+
+	+	−	□	−	□	−	□	−	□	−	+	+
+	+	□	−	□	−	□	−	□	−	□	+	+
+	×	●	●	●	×	●	×	●	×	●	●	+
+	●	×	●	×	●	×	●	×	●	×	●	+
+	●	●	×	●	●	●	×	●	●	●	×	+
+	○	○	○	○	○	○	○	○	○	○	○	+
+	−	−	−	−	−	−	−	−	−	−	−	+
+	○	−	○	−	○	−	○	−	○	−	○	+
+	+	○	●	○	●	○	●	○	●	○	+	+
+	+	Δ	Δ	Δ	Δ	Δ	Δ	Δ	Δ	Δ	+	+
+	+	+	□	□	□	□	□	□	□	+	+	+
+	+	+	+	●	●	●	●	●	+	+	+	+
+	+	+	+	+	+	+	+	+	+	+	+	+

Δ ○ ● × □ − +

Answer on page 48.

Baasil can't believe the pair are finally within his reach! But the situation is changing fast. Can you find ten differences between the two pictures below?

Answers on page 48.

Nothing can stop Baasil now . . . except these dominoes. He drops the longer legs and shoes to play his favorite game. Help him fill in the empty spaces.

Answers on page 48.

Answer on page 48.

The house is full, and Baasil is lost. Find him so he can keep following Hopper and Eggward.

Baasil's party selfie turned out really weird. Add some crazy elements to it!

Answer on page 48.

Time for a snack! Baasil wants to eat the flowers he is thinking about. Which basket should he choose?

Answer on page 48.

Oh no, rain! Baasil takes off his hat and builds an umbrella. Help him find the path with the fewest puddles on it.

Answer on page 48.

The sun is out, and Baasil closes his umbrella. He can see Hopper and Eggward up ahead! Look at the clues to mark their positions on the road with an X.

Answers on page 48.

THE EASTER SURPRISE

Eggward got tired of running, so he decided to wait for the end of the egg hunt in a field of tall grass beyond the orchard. Suddenly . . .

Answers

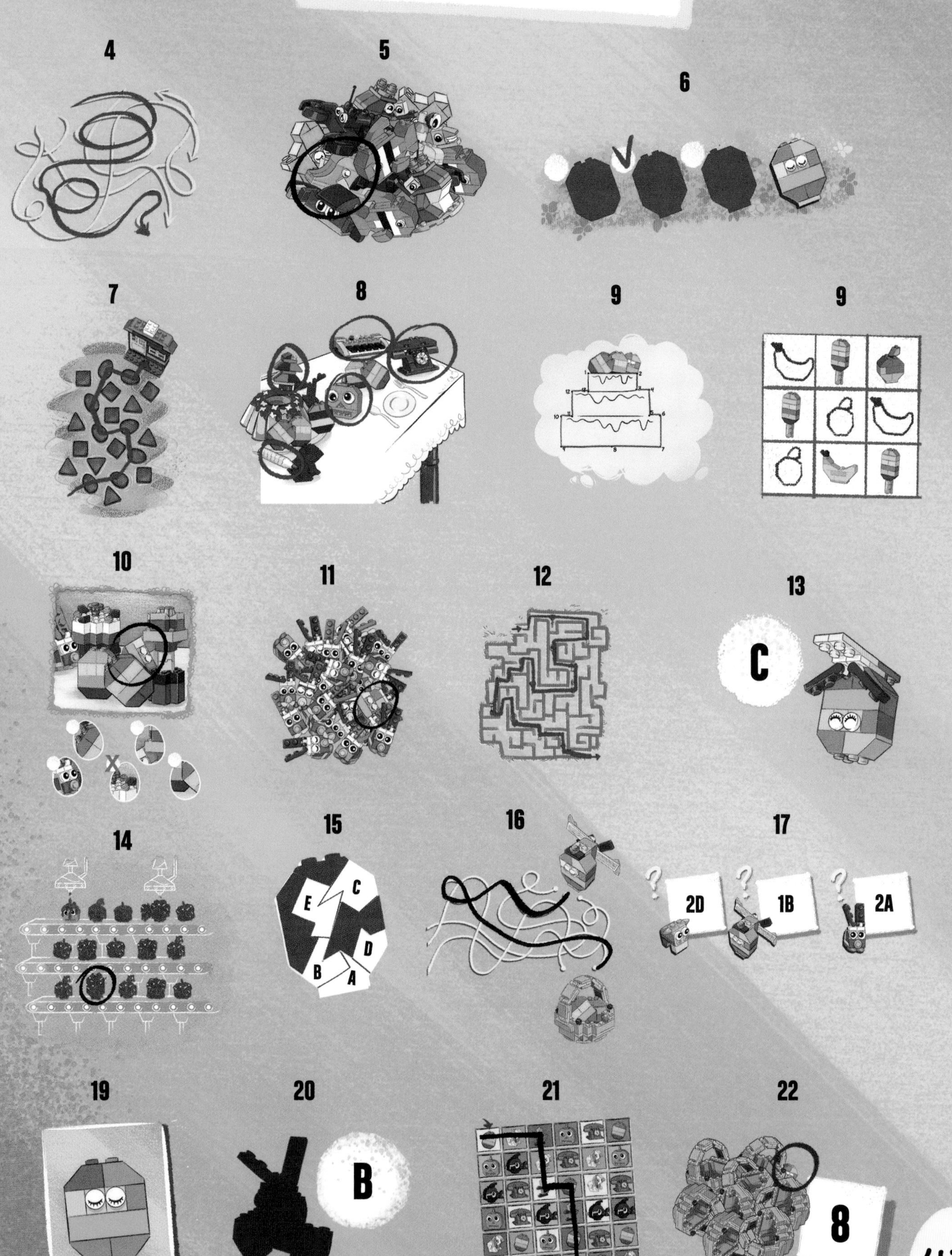

Answers

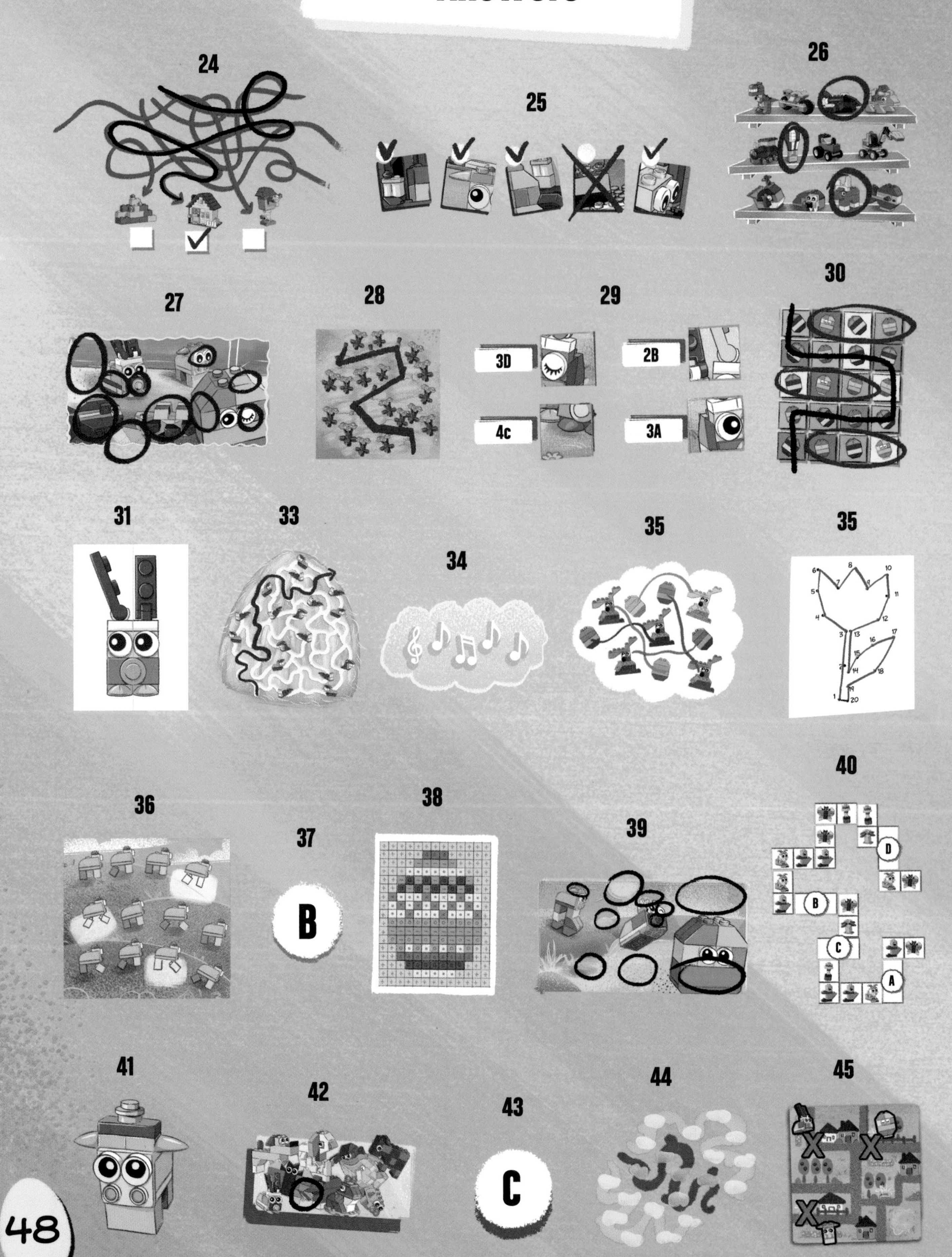
24
25
26
27
28
29
3D
2B
4c
3A
30
31
33
34
35
35
36
37
B
38
39
40
D
B
C
A
41
42
43
C
44
45
X
X
X